A DATE WITH THE MOUNTAIN MAN

HALLIE BENNETT

BOOKS BY THIS AUTHOR

All of Hallie's books feature a curvy heroine and a filthy-talking hero!
You can find them all at halliebennett.com!

For those who believe in soul mates.

PROLOGUE

RHYS

He did it.

King Bishop proposed to Hannah Welsh on New Year's Eve, and she said, "Yes."

Of course, she did.

King's a good man and deserves a solid partner like Hannah. I don't begrudge their happiness, especially after hearing about the scene that went down in Joe's Hardware on Christmas Eve—where King pretty much told the townspeople of Suitor's Crossing to boycott the store since the owner treated its long-time employees like shit.

But while I'm happy for the two of them, the whirlwind nature of their relationship gives me pause. Meeting someone and proposing to them a few weeks later?

No, thanks, I'm good.

At least you were able to finish the engagement ring in time or else the whole magical plan might have been ruined.

"Magical." An amused scoff rumbles from my chest because it's a romantic notion that's not for me. However, a good woman wouldn't be remiss.

I've lived alone for over a decade now, ever since I left my dad's house at eighteen, and the thought of coming home to a cabin filled with a woman's warmth stirs a craving deep inside my soul. But it's hard finding someone willing to overlook my bear-like size and gruff demeanor. Tougher to find one whose head isn't stuffed with dreams of happily-ever-after and Suitor's Crossing's very own love myth—a bunch of fantasy about *sparkin'* and *heart sparks*.

I don't need love; I prefer tangible things.

Like the hammer in my hand when I shape iron in my forge as the town's blacksmith.

Love comes and goes at will, a fleeting feeling. My mother taught me that.

But actions... Those actually prove something, and they can't be confused or misunderstood like the wisps of love. Actions produce results such as the ring I made for King—no mistaking what a gift like that means.

"Thanks again for completing the ring so quickly. I know it was short notice. But Hannah loves it, so I owe you big time. In fact..." King pauses until I look up from polishing a hand railing for the Pattersons over at High Ridge's Timber Bed & Breakfast. A sheepish look crosses his usually amiable features, and I wonder what's got him acting so oddly. "I signed you up for the dating app Luna Haven created. It's meant for locals, and I think it'll be good for you to branch out. Clearly, you're not having any luck finding love on your own."

"Luna? The woman named after a *Harry Potter* character?" I ask in disbelief. She's a sweet girl but takes a little too much inspiration from her namesake. "You're trusting my fate to an app she made? You know how I feel about online dating. It's a trash heap out there."

"Hey, don't diss the women around here. I'm starting to think you're the problem. You and your hang-ups about love and *heart sparks*." King crosses his arms and glares pointedly at me.

"A man's allowed to want what he wants. Nothing wrong with my decision to avoid the pitfalls of some made-up romantic legend. Just because you found your *heart spark*..." I stress the ridiculous moniker for people's soul mates in Suitor's Crossing. "Doesn't mean I want to. Or that I even believe in that crap. Surely, there must be a sane woman within a hundred-mile radius who feels the same."

King waves his phone in the air. "Well, I guess we'll see. I'll text you the login info, and you can adjust your bio if you want. Though Hannah helped me fill it out, and I think she did a damn good job."

"Of course, you'd think that," I mutter, but maybe his brash decision to sign me up for a dating app will prove fruitful. I've tried every other site to no avail.

What's one more?

CHAPTER ONE

B linking away the tears in my eyes, I toss my e-reader aside with a pained huff.

Another romance with a heroine who refuses to see what's right in front of her.

It's annoying to read these books with women rebuffing a man eager to love and please and protect them. *Others would gladly take your place*, I lament. *Wouldn't be so stupid or stubborn.* They'd be happy to accept what these women want to throw away and deny.

And it makes me cry because men don't want that girl.

They prefer the challenge.

Or the gorgeous supermodel who happens to be a size two.

I should know.

I'm the one who's always optimistic when it comes to relationships—never shy about my feelings. I want a forever kind of love and am upfront about it. Not to say I hit a guy over the head with wedding talk on our first date, but I don't like games and am terrible at playing hard to get.

My downfall, apparently.

Along with your shortness paired with an overabundance of curves.

At least, I assume that's my other issue since I don't have many date offers in the first place. Sighing, I stare up at my ceiling and contemplate the sad state of my love life right now.

A plaintive meow follows a furry paw swatting my stomach. Carrot whines again, desperate for his breakfast, and an unwilling smile tugs at my mouth. No time for pity parties when you have a starving cat on your hands.

"Alright, alright, I hear you... Let's get you fed." Whipping my covers off, I roll to a sitting position as Carrot hops down to the floor and races out the door, no doubt heading for his food bowl in the kitchen. My e-reader lays haphazardly on the edge of the mattress, and I snatch it up before it can fall, carefully placing it on my nightstand.

I'll read more later when I'm not in such a mood. When the heroine's antics won't bother me so much and I'll just be happy a girl like me finds love—even if it *is* in a fictional world.

"Dude, if I trip and die, you definitely won't be eating anytime soon." Because who knows when someone will come searching for me?

Okay, so my boss and friend, Shannon, will probably call when I don't show up for work, but still, it's the principle of the thing. A single woman living alone with her cat isn't as comforting as say a married woman living with her *husband* and cat, living with another human who can assist when said woman falls flat on her face. Unfortunately, logistics don't deter Carrot from winding between my legs as if it'll make me pour his food any faster.

Once the last piece of kibble clanks against the bowl, I lower it to the floor and start gathering my own breakfast: cold brew coffee with creamer and s'mores pop tarts. Because I'm classy and super healthy like that. My toaster glows red as it heats the two rectangles of deliciousness, and I lean against the counter to wait for them to finish, my gaze catching on the calendar hanging on the side of my fridge.

It's almost February.

A month meant for love, and one of the biggest times of the year for Suitor's Crossing. This town is known for its legend surrounding soul mates or as we like to call them, *heart sparks*.

There's a bridge where couples would go courting or *sparkin'* back in the day, and every single one of them knew the other was their *heart spark* by the end of their journey across the bridge, which is where the myth originated. The town even built a replica bridge for visitors to cross when they enter Suitor's Crossing to play up our special legacy of love.

"If only it were that easy..." I've lost count of how many times I've traveled over that bridge, yet here I am with no soul mate in sight.

Ping!

The notification bar appears on my phone indicating a match on the dating app I joined yesterday when I promised myself I wouldn't be alone again for Valentine's Day. "That was fast..." Hope blooms in my belly as the app opens to reveal a message from my mystery match.

FORGEDBYFIRE: *Hey, TheCarrotsMeow! Looks like we're a match. To be totally honest, I haven't had much luck on here so far, but if you're willing to meet, maybe my streak of bad luck will turn. P.S. What does your name mean? I can't decide if you really love carrots or what? LOL*

I grin and type out an explanation about my orange tabby while agreeing to a date. Usually, I prefer more conversation before jumping to meeting in person with a stranger, but he seems burnt out on the app. Might as well skip the niceties and get straight to the point of seeing if we're a good fit or not, especially since part of the app's charm is allowing users to not judge someone by their pictures.

It's meant to embody the true meaning of a blind date and to help local townspeople potentially find love where they never expected. Especially since Suitor's Crossing is a small town, making it difficult to meet someone new or view someone in a romantic light after knowing them for years. The goal of Luna's app, Suitor's Sparks, is to provide a solution for that particular problem.

"I should see if she's managed to use it for herself yet." Luna's always been eccentric. With a name based on a Ravenclaw from the *Harry Potter* series, it's hard to escape your destiny, but she's sweet, smart, and always up for an adventure. Traits that are impossible not to love about her.

Within a half hour, I scarf down my breakfast and dress before driving to Blushing Brides Boutique on Main Street where I've absolutely adored working for the past three years. Every bride's love story is unique and helping them find the perfect dress for their wedding day fulfills my sense of purpose. People might think it's silly to feel a sense of accomplishment from helping a bride buy a gown that's only worn one day, but as someone who never knew what she wanted to do with her life, it's a relief to have finally discovered something I love that complements my skills.

"Morning, Shannon," I call as I breeze through the back entrance, excited for our first client this morning: my best friend Hannah. Recently engaged after a whirlwind few weeks, she needs a dress equally fast since she and her groom don't want a prolonged engagement. Can't say I blame them.

I wouldn't be opposed to eloping if I found the love of my life so quickly either.

"Good morning! Ready for a new week?" Shannon's organizing a rack of dresses for Hannah to try when she arrives, and after dropping off my coat and purse, I join her.

"If you'd asked me earlier this morning, I would've said 'hell, no,' but..."

"But...?"

The doorbell chimes, and I smirk at the timing. "Saved by the bell. Let's wait for Hannah, so I can tell you both at the same time." We head toward the front of the store and exchange hellos with Hannah, who also brought Luna with her.

Small town, I think ruefully.

"Okay, I think we should start with the chiffon first, then we can go from there. You're going for a simple, classic look, right?"

Hannah nods and steps into the changing room with Shannon while Luna takes a seat on one of the velvet chaises for guests. "And while we're working on getting you into the gown, *Willow* can share her news," Shannon emphasizes my name, briefly poking her head out with a raised brow before retreating to assist Hannah.

"Oh, intriguing indeed. Tell us what's happened." Luna props one leg over the other and leans forward, anticipation lighting her eyes.

"Well, I signed up for your app yesterday and got a match this morning. He wants to meet tomorrow night at Daffodil's."

"This is so exciting!" Luna gushes. "You're the first person I know well enough to observe the app's work in progress."

"Who is it?" Hannah asks, her voice muffled.

"I don't know. There's not much to go on except for his bio since it's meant for blind dates. All I know is that he hasn't had much success with the app yet." Glancing toward Luna, I shrug in apology. "Sorry. I'm sure that's not what you want to hear."

She waves away my concern with purple-tipped fingers. "It's fine. It won't work for everyone, but if I can bring even one couple together, it'll be worth it. Maybe you'll be the lucky two!"

"Fingers crossed. My single season has to end eventually, right?"

"Right." Hannah steps out in a beautiful A-line gown covered in floating layers of pale chiffon. "Just look at me and King. Love happened in a matter of weeks for us after years of pining, and it can happen to you, too. We never know when we'll meet our *heart spark*. Yours could be at Daffodil's tomorrow night."

Giddy with optimism, I send up another prayer for this mystery man to be *my* man, then focus on Hannah. "Enough about me, though. You're the star today and that dress is lovely. How do you feel?"

Shannon and I listen as she details what she likes and dislikes, and we spend the rest of her appointment laughing and swooning over dresses until Hannah walks out in the perfect one, tears of joy glimmering in her eyes.

Someday that'll be me.

Someday.

CHAPTER TWO

RHYS

Dating sucks.

The women are nice enough, but none of them light a fire in my gut, especially when all of them get dreamy-eyed and wax poetic about love and *heart sparks*—a combination guaranteed to nix any chance we have together. It's why I'm about to delete this fucking app from my phone.

I don't know what King was thinking when he created an account for me.

Or why the hell I thought this app would be different from everything else I've tried to find a woman?

Instead of giving it one more chance, I should've trashed it and moved on with my life, but apparently, I'm a sucker for failure because when a new match came through, I set up a date anyway.

TheCarrotsMeow.

The name made me chuckle, which was a point in the woman's favor, and her cute explanation had me smiling. So I figured, "What the hell?" Maybe tonight won't be so terrible. Her bio listed the usual items like favorite books and movies, but other than a couple of random facts, she remains a mystery.

The sound of a truck pulling up to my forge distracts me from my thoughts, and I set down my current project to clean my hands before Austin Fielding enters.

"Hey, man." We shake hands in greeting as I lead him to the finished light fixtures he ordered for his bar, The Ole Aces. "Here they are. What do you think?"

Austin runs a careful hand over each piece composed of metal and wood. "They look really good. Better than what we have now, that's for sure, so thanks."

He bought the bar a year ago after the previous owner grew too old to maintain the business and the rowdy crowd it drew, so since then, Austin's been working on updating the interior while retaining its rustic charm.

"No problem. At least now I won't be afraid to play pool under one of those deathtraps you have hanging now." Every time I visit The Ole Aces, someone's standing on the old green bombazine-covered pool tables tinkering with the light overhead to ensure its stability.

"Yeah, I'll be thankful to not have that liability on my shoulders anymore," Austin mutters, running a hand through his long hair. "I shouldn't complain since I bought the old place for a song, but the renovations never seem to end. It's one thing after another."

"On the bright side, I think it matters more to you as the owner than your customers. We've been going there for years despite its rough edges; it matches our personalities," I joke, patting him on the back in encouragement. Owning a small business is tough—full of non-stop work—which I'm intimately familiar with. And I don't even manage a staff of people like Austin does. It's just me and the accountant I send my books to.

"I know, but for the sake of my sanity, I'll be glad when everything's done. The upside is we're close as long as nothing unexpected crops up. It helps that we've become a hub for the Reaper's Wolves MC. Those guys spend a shit-ton every single night."

"Pays to have good friends, huh?"

Austin and the motorcycle club's president are old military buddies which is why the club relocated to Suitor's Crossing last year. Snow heard his friend needed help, and like a true brother, he rode in with a club of men at his back ready to render aid.

The town wasn't too keen on the steel horse invasion, but for the most part, the men stick to themselves and don't cause too much trouble. They just run their strip club at the town's border and whatever other club shit they have on the agenda.

"Damn right. If you want to help me load these in my truck, I'll get going. I'd like to have these installed before the evening rush starts."

"Sounds good. Maybe I'll stop by later to see how they turned out." If my date goes awry, I definitely will need a beer to cheer me up.

Shaking off the negative prediction, I heft one of the light fixtures onto my shoulder and follow Austin outside to his truck. It shouldn't be this hard to find a woman. It's not like I'm asking for much. Just a lady I can take home to my dad and a hot-blooded wildcat I can fuck in my bed.

All while being someone who doesn't expect *heart sparks* and romantic shit that means fuck-all compared to what I can actually offer: security, companionship, *orgasms*.

Am I crazy for thinking those are worth more than frilly romantic sentiments?

DAMN, DAFFODIL'S IS crowded for a Wednesday night. I thought picking a day during the week would mean fewer witnesses to a potential disaster of a blind date, but clearly, I miscalculated.

Parking further down the block, I sneer at the large hearts decorating the street lamps. Already the town is poised to celebrate Valentine's Day all month long, eager to spread the *heart spark* legend to every tourist who stops by during this time. It's great marketing for our small town, though I wish everywhere I turned wasn't covered in red and pink. Especially since it's still fucking January.

This is why you stay hunkered down in your forge on the mountain. To avoid all the love shit.

I wouldn't exactly call myself a hermit, but my social circle revolves around a set couple of people: King, who is my nearest neighbor, the guys who own Olson-Keller Lumber & Construction where I source my wood supply, and Austin. Though the townspeople who've watched me grow up here prefer to think otherwise, always trying to force me into one social engagement or another.

A harsh wind nips my nose as I walk down the sidewalk, and I'm thankful for the beard protecting my cheeks. Living in the mountains is a lesson in braving the elements. Bitter winters can lead to being snowed in and rainy summers can result in mudslides. A man has to be prepared for every possibility.

Jazz music leaks out of Daffodil's as a couple leaves the restaurant, and my steps slow upon nearing the entrance. My mystery girl and I haven't exchanged many messages since setting up our date earlier. We confirmed the time and place and how we'll identify each other, but that's it.

I've got a red carnation in hand from the floral shop, something she suggested, while she'll be wearing white lace gloves—an odd choice in winter, but what do I know about women's fashion?

Absolutely nothing.

Hopefully, the impractical attire for this kind of weather isn't an indicator of other impractical beliefs of hers... like fairytales or *heart sparks*.

As I open the door to Daffodil's, there's a thump against my back, and a surprised squeak follows the crash of someone hitting the ground. *Seriously?* I'm a giant motherfucker, pretty hard to miss, yet somehow this person still managed to run into me—a pebble bouncing off the mountainside.

Words of annoyance stick in my throat as I whip around and see a woman lying on the concrete, the skirt of her dress tangled around her waist revealing thick thighs that I can't stop staring at.

They're dimpled and pale and perfect for squeezing as I eat—*Fuck!*

What's the matter with me?

I'm literally here for a blind date, yet I'm ogling the curvy bundle before me like she's the last piece of dessert at the buffet. And are those *cats* on her pussy?

The glimpse of her sense of humor brings a smile to my face as the possibility of her being my match crystallizes. What are the odds another woman loves orange tabbies enough to have playful kittens dancing between her thighs?

Surely not that high.

Which means *my* girl just ran into me like a fucking freight train of feminine heat, and tonight's off to a better-than-expected start.

Thank fuck.

CHAPTER THREE

WILLOW

There's a moment in every woman's life when she regrets wearing comfy cat-covered underwear rather than the sexy black panties tucked safely back home in her dresser drawer.

And for me, that moment is now—with my body sprawled on the sidewalk and the orange kittens I thought resembled Carrot prancing around on my cotton panties.

They were cute this morning. Punny even, but I failed to foresee running smack dab into a freaking oak tree and landing on my ass for all to view my clever choice of underwear.

"Here, take my hand. Are you okay?" A low baritone sweeps over me as a masculine hand comes into view. Glancing up—and up—my gaze finally lands on who I ran into: a giant of a man who looks like he can bench press my considerable weight with no problem. Heck, he could probably scale Black Mountain with me on his back without breaking a sweat.

Okay, that may be an exaggeration, but damn he's huge.

I've seen my fair share of mountain men wandering around Suitor's Crossing. Hard not to when you're nestled against a mountain range covered in rustic cabins, providing the ideal home for plaid-wearing, axe-toting lumberjacks. But this guy takes the cake.

He must not frequent Main Street often either because I've never seen him before.

"Are you okay?" He repeats, his hand still waiting for mine. Blushing in embarrassment at my blatant staring, my head dips in a nod as I accept his help.

Dashes of black mottle the side of his thumb, and I wonder at its origin. Is it grease? Is he a mechanic? Different scenarios race through my flustered brain as he helps me to my feet.

"I'm fine, thanks. Sorry for bumping into you. I should've paid better attention to where I was going." And not searching my purse for the white gloves I told my blind date I'd be wearing. *Speaking of which...* "I hate to literally hit and run, but I'm meeting someone and have to go. I'm already late and I'm sure he thinks I'm a flake and he doesn't even know me yet and..."

The stranger squeezes my hand, which I realize he's still holding, amusement creeping into his brown eyes.

Damn, I was rambling.

Now, I'm breathless from over-talking... and falling... and this hot man's rough palm cradling my smaller one. It's a lot for a girl who's already nervous about meeting a stranger for her date tonight.

"Breathe, kitten." His other hand smooths a caught strand of hair off my forehead, and I shiver at the intimate touch. "You're worth the wait... *TheCarrotsMeow*?"

Shock burns away some of the embarrassment coursing through my veins. Just my luck—crashing into my potential *heart spark* like an uncontrolled vehicle flying down the highway. "*ForgedByFire*? You're my match?"

He bends to pick up a slightly crushed red carnation, offering it to me with a confident grin. "Guilty."

Heart sparks.

Suitor's Crossing's legend of love come to life.

I've always believed in it. Envied the happy couples who had it. But in the back of my mind, there's been a well of doubt that's deepened each time another one of my friends found love, while I settled for the rare match on an app.

Doesn't matter now.

Because I only need one match.

The match.

And I might have just found him.

Reluctantly pulling my hand from his, my chin ducks down as I focus on straightening my skirt and brushing off any lingering dirt clinging to my backside. "What's your name? I'm Willow."

"Rhys."

Wait, that sounds familiar. I pause and glance upward to meet his friendly gaze. "Rhys? As in the guy who made Hannah Welsh's engagement ring?"

"Yeah, I'm friends with King. I'm guessing you're friends with her?"

I nod, marveling at small-town magic, and motion toward Daffodil's which looks pretty full. "Should we grab a table inside? We can talk more when my legs aren't about to freeze to death in this skirt."

"Well, we can't have that." Rhys smiles and steps back for me to go ahead of him. "Ladies first."

Scooting by him in the narrow entryway, my back grazes his broad chest, and a shiver of awareness erupts over my skin. This is the first time a man's had this immediate effect on my body, and it's exhilarating.

Brides have gushed about those first sparks when they met their future husband—love at first sight. And a lot of the romances I read feature a moment when the heroine just *knows* the hero is meant for her.

But it seemed like an impossibility for me considering my past of lackluster dates. However, maybe my luck is changing because I definitely feel a spark with Rhys.

Like he's the guy for me.

Intuitively. No rhyme or reason to it. Just a gut feeling.

Don't get ahead of yourself. Try talking with the man first.

A waitress guides us to a table for two, and we take seats opposite each other. Poor Rhys squeezes behind the table, his massive body not meant for an intimate setting like Daffodil's.

"Are you gonna be comfortable here? We can go somewhere else if you'd like," I suggest. Truthfully, it's a bit of a tight fit for my large hips and belly, as well, especially with the man behind me pushing his chair further back, edging into my space.

"While I definitely underestimated Daffodil's popularity tonight, I'll manage. Let's just hope they don't sit someone behind me because I'm not sure there's gonna be room for them to pull the chair out, let alone sit." Rhys glances backward at a tiny table shoved into the corner.

We're at the rear of the restaurant where it looks like they tried to make every last inch count, despite the lack of room for maneuvering around. "I'd rather spend time chatting with you rather than searching town for another dinner spot anyway."

"As long as you're comfortable..." A flush of pleasure warms my cheeks as I fidget in my chair. "So, Mr. ForgedbyFire, how'd you become a blacksmith? The last time I heard about that job was in a historical rom—novel."

A romantic novella by Tessa Dare almost spilled from my mouth before I caught myself in time. I wouldn't say I'm embarrassed about my preference for reading romance novels, but it's not something I lead with on dates. It tends to freak guys out like I'm asking them to live up to astronomical standards. You know... because asking for respect and orgasms in a loving relationship is too much to expect from a man these days.

A mental eye roll springs forth, and I study Rhys. He doesn't look like the kind of guy who gets freaked out by much. He's got that whole "I'm as sturdy as a mountain and can withstand whatever comes my way" vibe. But looks can be deceiving.

"That's where I first learned about it, too, actually. A history book in seventh grade. I've always liked working with my hands and dealing with molten metal sounded badass. So, I found an apprenticeship in Seattle after high school before moving back here to start my own business."

"So, you grew up here?" I'm always a little envious of the people who are from Suitor's Crossing. It's an idyllic town, perfect for families with its tight-knit community, and I wish I had something similar while I was growing up.

Unfortunately, my childhood was spent moving around the country following my dad as his job uprooted our family every few years. Hard to plant roots or befriend a community when you're leaving right around the time you start to feel settled.

"Yep, born and raised. My dad used to be a foreman with a timber company near High Ridge," he explains after we give our dinner order to a harried waitress.

"What about your mom?"

A shadow crosses Rhys's face and his lips thin into a flat line. "Don't know. She left us when I was two."

"Oh, I'm so sorry. I shouldn't have..."

"No, it's fine." He shakes his head. "It's a reasonable question since I mentioned my dad. Besides, her leaving wasn't all bad. It taught me a valuable lesson at a young age." Rhys pauses, his gaze studying me, and I get the impression he's contemplating whether or not to share this lesson with me.

My belly seizes into a knot as a sense of foreboding creeps in. *Get a grip, Willow. It's not going to be bad.* But I can't shake the feeling he's about to impart a major facet of his life—one that may put an end to us before we've even begun.

"My parents were high school sweethearts, believed in the stupid myth about Suitor's Crossing and *heart sparks*. Until my mom decided she didn't love my dad anymore and took off with another man. Apparently, *he* was her *heart spark*, not Dad." Rhys spits out the words *heart spark* with enough venom to kill, and a shudder of concern sets my heart to beating double-time. "Which is why I don't believe in the bullshit about *heart sparks* or love. It's not real."

Not real.

The conviction in his voice is an arrow straight through my chest.

My potential *heart spark* doesn't believe in love.

Can that even be possible?

Told you not to get ahead of yourself...

CHAPTER FOUR

RHYS

Dinner proves to be a quiet affair after I drop the bomb about my mom and *heart sparks*. Probably not the best decision to lay it all out there for Willow when she hardly knows me, but it would've been said eventually. This way she knows where I stand, and we can hopefully move past it.

Because unlike the women of my past, I don't want to dismiss Willow or continue searching for the right woman.

I want *her*.

Even if it means hammering out how to work together when I'm ninety percent sure she probably believes the exact opposite of me. I mean she told me she works at a damn bridal boutique when our food arrived. It doesn't get much more obvious that she's a strong believer in everything Suitor's Crossing is known for.

"Sorry for springing the love thing on you so soon. Didn't mean to get into such heavy shit on our first date." I try to gauge where her head's at, but her expression remains carefully neutral as she finishes the last bite of her burger.

"I'm glad you told me. I'm just trying to process what exactly it means." She piles her used utensils and a balled-up napkin on top of her plate before setting it aside and leaning forward. "My parents weren't the model couple for relationships, and I've never been in love before, but that doesn't mean I don't believe in it."

"But you weren't actively avoiding it," I point out.

"No, more like it was avoiding *me*... Though you bring up an interesting point." Willow rests her chin on a closed fist and bends even closer, forcing her tits to swell above the neckline of her blouse. Unable to resist the tempting sight, my eyes drop down for a moment before I force myself to raise them again and listen to what she's saying. "To avoid something, you have to believe it exists. And you said you don't believe in love at all." She smirks as if her knight just took my queen to make checkmate, and I shake my head, preparing to disabuse her of the notion.

"I don't, but I avoid women who do."

"So I won't be seeing you again after tonight?" Willow challenges.

She's got me there.

"That's up to you." Not entirely true, but it sounds better than saying *I'm keeping you no matter what*. "Are you okay being with someone that doesn't fit the fairytale in your mind? Because even if I can't promise you *heart sparks*, I can promise respect, fidelity, and more—tangible things that matter."

Willow's teeth bite into her bottom lip, and I stare transfixed as the soft pink slowly turns a darker red. Goddamn, she's pretty. My cock's been hard throughout our entire dinner, and I wish we could forgo the topic of love and head straight toward the subject of me pinning her against my truck, claiming that pouty little mouth of hers for my own.

"First of all, you don't know what I've envisioned for my future. Yes, I work with lovestruck brides, and maybe I love fairytales, but that doesn't mean I'm stupid. Real life and relationships require work," she huffs, putting me in my place, which only serves to rouse my desire higher. "So, how about we compromise? We agree to not rule out the possibility of love or the possibility of a successful relationship without it. After all, we're still practically strangers. This could all be a moot point once I learn you like pineapple on your pizza," she teases, a sparkle of mischief diffusing some of the seriousness filling her blue eyes.

A reluctant chuckle rumbles from my throat. Normally, if a woman suggested a compromise, I'd refuse, knowing full well it was a ploy to try and get me to change my mind rather than for her to come around to my way of thinking. But with Willow, I'm willing to try whatever she wants to make this work.

Besides, she's right. We don't know each other well—even if my gut *is* telling me to lock her down for the long haul.

It's not like I've never been wrong before.

An unwanted comparison to my parents pops into my head. How they met and my dad fell instantly.

You're not a dumb high schooler. You're not naive enough to equate lust with love just because of a stupid town myth.

No, I'm a grown man who's attracted to Willow. Physically, yes, but also to her sense of humor. Two things that are already more sensible than romantic love.

"Deal. Should we shake on it?" I offer my hand over the table, and she confidently shakes it before gathering her purse. The strap is wedged between her chair and the person behind her's seat as the crowd at Daffodil's has swelled over the past hour. Yanking it free, Willow turns back to me with an exasperated puff of breath.

"Now that we've settled one thing tonight, why don't we pay for this and take a walk down Main Street? It's pretty with all of the Valentine's Day decorations lighting it up."

"Pretty's not how I'd describe it but sure." She reaches for her wallet, but I wave her off, dropping a few folded bills on the table to cover our tab along with a generous tip. Our waitress deserves it with all the customers she's dealing with tonight.

A brisk gust of wind hits us in the face once we exit the warmth of Daffodil's, and immediately, I'm questioning our decision to meander outside with Willow in a skirt. "Are you going to be warm enough for a walk? We can probably find someplace to sit inside. Or you can take my coat for extra protection."

"I'm good, thanks. Walking will keep me warm enough." She stuffs her hands in her jacket pockets and smiles as I move between her and the street.

Red hearts grace every lamp post, while pink streamers and Edison lights crisscross the street. The tinny sound of a ballad echoes in the air, the hidden speakers set in planters losing their battle against a wintry howl.

"You must hate this time of year," Willow observes from my side as she takes in all the over-the-top decorations before sparing a glance of sympathy my way.

Shrugging, I study the familiar adornments lining each shop on Main Street. "Hate's a strong word. It gets annoying sometimes, but that's why I stay at home or in my forge most of the time. Tell me more about yourself. All I know is that you have a cat named Carrot and work at the bridal boutique."

"Because those are two of the most important things in my life. Blushing Brides Boutique is where I found my passion—helping women look and feel their best for one of the best days of their lives. In fact, I helped Hannah find her wedding dress this morning. Other than that, there's not much to tell. I love working with brides, adore Carrot, and read in my spare time."

"I don't know Hannah super well, just what I've experienced when she worked at the hardware store, but King's obsessed, so it's obvious she's a good one. What about Carrot? Did you adopt him?" I ask, thinking about my dad's old cat, Elmer. He was dropped off at the shelter with a broken leg that needed amputation, and Dad couldn't resist the three-legged rascal after deciding he wanted a companion at home when I moved out.

"He is. They said he was about three years old when I got him, and it's been two years since then. He's basically all about food and cuddles."

"Not a bad life." I wouldn't mind cuddling Willow's lush curves either.

A jovial laugh tinkles through the air, and her obvious amusement warms me from the inside out. I always want to see that look of pure joy on her face.

Settle down. It's too soon to jump into forever thinking.

But I can't help the pull Willow has on me. Can't deny the possessive feelings or hungry need building inside my body.

"Nope, not at all. If only we could all live as simply." The town square comes into view with its statue of one of the founders at the center of a closed fountain. Willow hops onto the concrete ledge, bringing her nearer to my height though the top of her head still only reaches my chin.

"Careful," I warn, instinctively wrapping my hands around her hips for stability. Her arms loop around my neck as her head tilts slightly back, and my blood heats at the implication.

Willow studies my expression as if searching for an unspoken question before it seems she makes up her mind about something—an entire silent conversation occurring while my mind whispers prayer after prayer that this leads to where I'm hoping.

"Kiss me, Rhys," she finally rasps, a shy sultriness entering her voice. "I think I need a little more heat to combat this February chill."

"Whatever you need, kitten." My head lowers until our mouths meet in a swirl of steam and passion, mutual groans of satisfaction ringing in the air. I squeeze her soft body tighter to mine, enjoying the plush give in her curves as they conform to my firmer muscles.

Yes, this is what I want.

Willow—a flesh and blood woman whose kiss is as hot as the fire that burns in my kiln.

Physical attraction, real and tangible.

Who needs a romantic fantasy when I can have this?

CHAPTER FIVE

WILLOW

The winter cold fades as Rhys's warmth seeps through the layers of my clothing. I've never felt small in my life, yet in his arms—with his strength wrapped around me—I feel petite, a delicate creature safe and under his protection.

It's a heady thought considering how unattainable such a thing has been for most of my life. My body's always been short and chubby and never featured in movies or those cute video clips of girls jumping into their boyfriends' arms.

Realistically, I figured it was too much to hope that I'd find a man able to make me feel so secure and light—not a burden to lift even for a moment of overwhelming joy.

But with Rhys...

Another shiver of pleasure cascades downward to center on my core as his hold tightens, bringing me up to my tiptoes as if I really am as dainty as the "kitten" endearment he keeps calling me.

His mouth demands mine submit while his beard scrapes my cheeks, electrifying the fine nerve endings, and a muted moan hums in my throat.

"Damn, kitten..." Rhys murmurs against my lips. "You're too sweet for words. I can't believe our paths haven't crossed before now." He nibbles his way down my neck, hot licks of his tongue leaving behind damp patches that burn in the February air—a study in extremes that sends my senses spiraling deeper into desire.

"That'll change with our friends marrying." King and Hannah's marriage is bound to bring Rhys and I together more often, and it seems like fate that we would've met eventually. That even if a dating app hadn't matched us, destiny or some other higher power would've ensured our meeting.

Heart sparks.

"It'll change because now I know you exist. Know the taste of your pretty mouth. The intoxicating honey scent of your skin." He crushes me impossibly closer, and I yearn to rub my sensitive nipples across his chest, to gain any sort of relief from the ache he's built inside me, but I'm locked in his immovable embrace. "You're in my blood now, kitten, and there's no escaping."

Goodness... Is it possible to come just from a few roughly spoken words?

My thighs clench together as the throbbing in my clit intensifies. Rhys puts my book boyfriends to shame, and I've got some good ones, not gonna lie. But here's a hot-blooded mountain of a man basically claiming me as his own—this is the stuff my dreams are made of.

"Kiss me again," I pant, desperate for his possession. Rhys growls before complying, sweeping me off the edge of the fountain and walking us backward until my back hits the brick of a building.

Town hall, probably, my mind absentmindedly provides.

I'm not sure how long we stay there, locked together for every citizen of Suitor's Crossing to witness our frantic passion. All I know is that by the time he escorts me back to my car,

I'm sweating as if it's summertime instead of winter, my lips are swollen from his harsh treatment, and my vibrator is about to get the workout of its life when I arrive home.

"Good night, kitten. We'll talk more tomorrow." Rhys pats my bottom before landing a gentle kiss on my forehead. He watches me drive away, and in my haze of lust, I completely forget about the potential pitfalls ahead of us—*our differing opinions about love.*

"WHAT DO YOU MEAN HE doesn't believe in love?" Shannon asks in shock the next morning when I relay the details of my date with Rhys last night, finally able to think clearly after a night of self-given orgasms and fantasizing about my potential *heart spark.*

Due to a last-minute cancellation this morning, we're busy sorting dresses for the next appointment in an hour, which gives us plenty of time to discuss my conundrum of a date.

"Just what I said. His mom did a real number on him, and now he's all 'love's not real.'" I lower my voice in a sad impersonation of Rhys's sexy baritone and sigh. "His points are valid as far as offering respect and security in a relationship, though I'm not sure those are more important than love, more like they're on equal footing."

"Hmmm... It kind of sounds like he shows love through acts of service rather than words." The reference to one of the five love languages doesn't surprise me. Shannon's been reading a ton of relationship books lately in preparation for her marriage to her fiance, Tim. "Like Rhys wouldn't say he's showing love but his actions prove otherwise. When you think about it, wouldn't you rather actions over words anyway?"

Considering this new perspective, my eyes scan the strapless gown in my hand absentmindedly. "Yeah... I would, especially since it's better than the other way around—all words but no actions to back them up. Guess I would just like both."

Because if we're talking love languages, one of mine is words of affirmation. My family was never big on compliments, no matter what I accomplished, so it's only natural that I'm hungry for some kind of positive feedback.

You should probably schedule another session with Dr. Walton.

As if I haven't gone over this need with my therapist a thousand times already.

Shannon shrugs and adds another dress to the rack. "I get that. Though I still think it's too early to even bring love into the equation. Y'all move too fast for me, both you and Hannah."

"Says the woman who waited five years for her boyfriend to finally propose. I don't know how you did it."

"Trust me, it wasn't always easy. But at least we know each other now. Tim's been with me through the holidays, met my family, and vice versa. No more surprises."

Sounds kind of boring to me, but I keep the thought to myself. If it's what Shannon wants, then that's her prerogative. "Well, I don't see Rhys proposing anytime soon, so rest easy," I tease, unsure how I'd even react to a marriage proposal.

Who are you kidding?

If he got down on one knee and promised me forever, I'd say yes so fast, I'd probably break some Guinness world record.

Yep, definitely schedule an appointment with Dr. Walton.

It's not that I'm so desperate I'd agree to marry anyone who proposed, but Rhys is different. He makes *me* feel different. Like I'm precious to him, desirable. And I can't ignore the instinct saying he's my *heart spark*.

"Good," Shannon huffs, darting a pointed glance in my direction. "In other news, Tim's only available to tour our wedding venue on the thirteenth, which means I won't be able to cover our booth for Hearts Ablaze. Are you alright handling it by yourself?"

The week of Suitor's Crossing's annual festival to celebrate Valentine's Day is one of our biggest moneymakers. So many people flood Main Street to check out the carnival and booths, and we meet a ton of brides who gladly take our business cards.

"Sure, I'll be fine, and if worse comes to worst, I'll just call Hannah or Luna to see if they can help." The bell rings announcing our next client's arrival, and Shannon steps back to assess the gowns we've pulled.

"Thanks! I hate leaving you alone during one of the busiest times of the year for us, but it's been difficult working around Tim's schedule. He doesn't really care about any of the wedding planning stuff either, which makes it extra tough." A note of dejection enters her tone, making me wish I could ask if everything's alright between them, but before I'm able to respond, Shannon's gone to greet our client.

I'll check in on her later.

I'd hate for there to be trouble brewing between her and Tim, but it wouldn't come as a surprise based on what I've seen from her fiance.

"Kelsey, this is Willow. She'll be helping us find your perfect wedding gown." Shannon returns with the bride and her small entourage of friends and family. Stowing away my concern for another time, I smile in greeting, focusing on doing my job rather than hypothesizing about the status of Shannon's relationship.

Besides, you have your own relationship to think about.

With Rhys—the man who rejects the possibility of *heart sparks*.

CHAPTER SIX

RHYS

Raucous laughter rises from a table in the back where a couple of members of the Reapers Wolves MC are enjoying their beer and a game of darts. Checking my phone again for the time, I shake my head and sigh, taking a long drag of the bottle in front of me.

"Expecting someone?" Austin asks from behind the bar. It's a Thursday night at The Ole Aces with customers busy searching for greasy food and alcohol, and I should be home relaxing after a hard day's work, preferably with Willow by my side.

"Just King, but he's late. I'm guessing he got caught up with Hannah." Which I can't blame him for. If Willow were free tonight, I'd choose to be with her rather than agreeing to hang with King to discuss custom wedding bands for him and his bride.

Austin laughs. "Bet you're right... I envy him. A good woman can be hard to find." *Especially when you've got a face like mine.* He doesn't say the words aloud, but they hang in the air nonetheless. During his time in the military, an explosion left him with severe burns that forced him out of active duty. The visible scars on his face aren't pretty, and I'm guessing the women of his acquaintance have made it abundantly clear to him that it's an issue.

Superficial bitches.

"The right one will come along if that's what you want. You're a good man."

"Like a woman will come along for you, too? How's that app working out? King mentioned it to me the other day, but I told him if he signed me up, I'd ban him from the bar."

Memories of my night with Willow heat my blood. I can almost taste the sugary sweetness of her mouth still. *And the fucking dreams I've had...* My cock hardens remembering this morning's scene where Willow woke me with her soft mouth.

Too bad you had to make do with your hand when you woke up.

"Well, I met someone. I'm just not sure it'll work out. She's all about romantic lovey dovey shit, and I'm not." Though that didn't exactly stop us from making out like a couple of teens. It required all of my strength to pull away and let her go home instead of snatching her up in my arms and hauling her back to my cabin.

"I forgot about your issue with love. Why is that anyway?"

"Because he's lived in Suitor's Crossing for too long," King interjects as he plops onto the bar stool next to mine. "Sorry, I'm late. Had to help Hannah with something."

Snorting, I imagine what he had to help his fiance with was something along the lines of what I'd like to do with Willow—fuck her luscious curves into exhaustion. Austin slides a fresh bottle of beer King's way before asking, "What's living in Suitor's Crossing have to do with anything? This town's all about love."

"And that's the problem." King tips the lip of his bottle toward Austin. "Rhys here has become too cynical due to being surrounded by *heart sparks* constantly, instead of going the logical way and trusting in its power."

"If tonight's gonna turn into psychoanalyzing me, then I'm gonna head home where I can live in peace."

"And quiet."

"Cold and alone," Austin adds, grinning with King.

"Both of you are ridiculous." Shaking my head at their ribbing, I change the subject, bombarding King with a litany of questions before he has a chance to continue in his current vein. "Are you ready to go over ring designs? Will I get more than a few weeks to complete these, or will it be another rush job?"

He takes the hint and launches into his ideas for the wedding bands while Austin retreats to fill other customer orders. *Thank fuck.* I've never been grilled so much about my relationship status or thoughts on love until now.

Fucking heart sparks.

WILLOW: *Just finished with another bride and about to grab lunch with Luna. How about you?*

Unable to resist a stupid grin from forming on my face at the *Harry Potter* Luna meme she sent, I fill her in on my latest project before asking if she'd like to have dinner together tonight. It's been a few days since our date, and I'm starved for my girl—an unexpected position to be in.

I've never felt this drive to be near someone as much as I do with Willow. Somehow she's become a hive of honeyed goodness, and I'm the bee buzzing merrily in her direction, powerless to refuse her call.

WILLOW: *Works for me! My place at 7? Carrot would like to meet you. ;)*

A swift chuckle follows the pronouncement, imagining an orange fluffball cozied up in Willow's arms.

ME: *Sounds good, kitten. See you and Carrot then.*

The afternoon flies by after our conversation as a calm settles over me while melding pieces of an ornate gate together. Everything feels right in this moment. I've got a successful career I enjoy and a woman I could see myself spending forever with. Hell, I'm even starting to think I'd be willing to entertain her ideas of love if it means keeping her—a huge fucking step for me. Of course, wariness and doubt remain in the back of my mind, since love and *heart sparks* are fickle things.

She could say she loves me only to turn around and change her mind.

Willow's not Mom.

A distinction I understand logically, but what do I really know about her? What I've seen so far I'm obsessed with, but maybe that's just a first date facade. Maybe that's not who Willow really is.

The possibility plagues my thoughts until I knock on Willow's apartment door a few hours later. When she opens the door with a beaming smile, my worry evaporates like morning dew under the sun, and conviction grows in my heart—she's the real deal. Genuine and sweet. Not a disingenuous bone in her curvy little body.

My mind should require more proof, yet it agrees with everything my gut's telling me.

"Come in!" Willow waves me inside where warmth immediately envelops me along with the scent of steak. "Would you like something to drink?"

Damn, I should've offered to bring wine or something. *Or flowers.* But it slipped my mind amidst all of my concerns about a serious relationship with Willow, not to mention my inexperience when it comes to proper dating protocol. Usually things never progress to the point where the knowledge is necessary.

Because flowers or candy are unnecessary when you're just fucking?

I sound like an asshole.

A sliver of shame twists in my gut, and I wonder if King didn't have a point when he accused me of being the problem instead of the women I dated. Maybe I've been taking this whole avoidance of love and romance thing too far when all I really needed to do was be open-minded and use common sense.

It feels like I'm on the verge of realizing something important—life-altering—until the train of thought is lost because of a purring cat at my feet. Lowering to my haunches, I smooth a palm down its silky fur, eliciting an even louder purr of contentment.

"He likes you." Willow bends down to scratch behind the feline's ears. "Carrot, this is Rhys. Rhys, Carrot." Her formal introduction of us is adorable, and I can't help wrapping a hand behind her neck and tugging her close enough so my lips can brush across hers.

"Thanks for the intro, kitten. I like him, too. Do you need help with anything in the kitchen?" Perhaps I can make up for not bringing anything as an offering.

"Nope, I'm good. Just relax while I plate our food."

Studying Willow's home, it's obvious she wasn't kidding when she listed the top three priorities in her life: working with brides, Carrot, and reading. Bookshelves line one wall, some shelves dipping under the weight of colorful titles, and I make a note to come back to reinforce them before they completely fail. Photos of her and Carrot grace several spots around the room along with group shots with her friends.

Her personality is written into the space—an undeniable expression of Willow.

"You've got a nice place," I say, moving toward the dining table once I see she has everything set for dinner.

"Thanks! It took me a while to figure out what I wanted to do. Growing up, we moved around a lot, so it kind of felt like a waste of time to hang pictures and personalize a place," she explains while cutting her steak into manageable pieces. The spread before us is way more than I expected but definitely appreciated. Thick steaks, baked potatoes, corn on the cob—a smorgasbord of comfort food awaits me, a home-cooked meal like I haven't had in ages.

"Why'd your family move so much?" I'm curious about her parents and their relationship. She said they weren't the model couple on our first date, but what exactly did that mean?

"My dad was a campaign consultant. We were always traveling to his next candidate's county or state to help them win their election. It didn't matter how big or small it was either." Willow chews slowly, a resigned look shadowing her usually optimistic features. "That's a lot of elections and a lot of uprooting our lives."

"I'm sorry to hear that." Reaching across the table, I squeeze her fisted hand. "Did you have siblings to ease the burden of starting over so often?"

"A younger brother, Jacob. He followed in Dad's footsteps, so I hardly see him anymore. My family and I aren't super close, which is why I love Suitor's Crossing. Everyone declares you family once you're accepted into the fold."

She's right. While we have a couple small town cliques, for the most part we accept people into the community as long as they're friendly. *And sometimes when they're not,* I admit to myself, remembering the times I've dismissed an invitation or ignored a phone call.

Geez, I really have been an asshole.

I don't think I realized how much of an impact my mom's leaving had on me outside of romantic relationships. Sure, I'm not the most outgoing guy, but have I really distanced myself from the people of my hometown because of a misguided belief they'd turn on me? Abandon me?

Fuck. This is too heavy to deal with now.

"And you've built your own little support system here, too, with Hannah and Luna, right?" She'd mentioned in an earlier message how she's friends with the eclectic creator of Suitor's Sparks.

"Yep, along with Shannon, who's technically my boss but feels more like an older sister most days."

"I'm glad you've found your people, and now you can count me among them." Because no matter what happens, I don't foresee being able to let Willow go. There's a deep-seated knowledge in my gut that she's it for me. Some may call it a *heart spark*, but I know those are too unpredictable to be what I'm feeling.

This intuition is too real, prompting all sorts of ideas of possessiveness, of the need to protect her at all costs, to fulfill her every desire. It's an instinct written in immovable stone.

When Willow begins to clear the table, I try to take over since she cooked, but she refuses to accept my help—just continues to the kitchen sink where she starts rinsing off our plates.

"It's only fair I clean when you cooked," I mutter, caging her against the counter with my hands on either side of her hips. Water splashes on her shirt as she jerks, and the cotton fabric quickly adheres to her round tits.

"This... This isn't about fair." The stuttering sentence spills from her mouth in a nervous warble. "You're my guest, and I don't mind cleaning up. It's just rinsing these off to put in the dishwasher." Her hands tremble as she grabs another plate beside the sink and runs it under the rush of warm water.

"In that case, I suppose I'll have to show my appreciation for you and dinner a different way." My promise whispers over her ear before I kiss right below it, reveling in the immediate softening of her body as she leans into me.

Slowly, I skim my hands over her hips and breasts until I reach the top of her damp blouse, unbuttoning the tiny pearl beads to reveal a pink flush staining her chest. Our heavy breathing mingles together as the plate Willow's holding clatters into the sink.

"You don't... I mean if you want..."

"Trust me, I *want*."

The limp sides of her shirt hang open as my rough palms slide over her smooth skin to cup the heavy weight of her breasts over the serviceable bra she's wearing. I like that she kept it practical, wearing something meant to actually do its job rather than some flimsy scrap of fabric whose only purpose is to look pretty.

Willow's gorgeous enough without extra ornamentation.

"I want to know what it sounds like when you come on my fingers," I growl, tracing the curve of her belly with one finger before going lower and undoing her jeans so I can freely cup her hot pussy. "I want to know what it looks like for pleasure to overtake your sweet little body. Does the blue of your eyes turn to midnight? Does this endearing blush of yours deepen to burgundy? I need to know, kitten."

"Rhys..." Willow tilts her head back, and I snare her mouth in a fiery kiss, staking my claim like I've wanted to all evening. She tastes like the heart-shaped cookies we had for dessert—rich, sugary deliciousness—and I can't get enough.

Her breath catches as I push aside her panties to delve between her slick folds, sticky arousal already easing my passage. "Damn, kitten. Is all this for me?" My thumb circles her clit, and she arches into the rhythmic stroking.

"Mmm... You have quite the effect on my body," she admits breathily. "I've never felt this strongly for anyone before, and it doesn't make much sense considering how we were strangers a few days ago."

"Doesn't matter how long we've known each other, kitten. Our bodies recognize the other." It's the closest I've ever come to accepting anything resembling *heart sparks*—not that I think that's what this is—but there's definitely a connection between us, one that defies logic.

It's called lust.

True, but it's more than my attraction to her sexy curves or beautiful smile. It's the kindness in her eyes and gestures. The quirky humor she surprises me with. Willow's curves fit the gaps in my life; I know the truth of it deep in my bones.

I nip the side of her neck and pinch one of her pert nipples after releasing it from a bra cup, and warm heat gushes onto the fingers I'm pumping into her clenching cunt. "Eyes on me, Willow. Don't deny me what I want. Every inch of you belongs to me; your every orgasm is mine. Now, come for me, soak my fingers with this wet pussy."

The sky blue of her irises darken like I predicted as a muted cry falls from her lips, her body quaking in my arms as she obeys my command.

Goddamn, she's perfect.

"You come so beautifully, kitten," I praise, nuzzling her cheek as my movements slow, letting her body ease down from its high.

"*Meow.*"

We both look down in surprise to see Carrot staring up at us in annoyance. Glancing at each other, a beat of silence hangs in the air before we burst into laughter, an odd release after Willow's intense orgasm.

"I think he's jealous about not getting enough attention." She giggles, turning to bury her head in my chest, while I work on getting her clothes back to the way they were after licking my fingers clean of her sweet arousal.

"Should we move to the couch and indulge him? Maybe watch a movie?"

"And cuddle?" she asks hopefully, a bright smile blinding me with its radiance. I've never been one to cuddle, but with Willow? Hell yes, I can get behind holding her soft body against mine for two hours straight. "Or I could..." She peeks down at the hard erection testing the limits of my jeans.

How I would love to have her finish me off—with her mouth, her hands, however she desired—but we don't have to rush, I don't want to push things further when there's time to explore.

"Nah, I'm good. Tonight was about you. And now it's gonna be about Carrot." Bending down, I pick up the attention-seeking feline, his tail swishing back and forth across my arms.

"Are you sure...?"

"Positive." I grab her hand and tug her toward the living area. "What movie should we watch?"

Willow bites her lip but doesn't press the issue. *Thank god for small mercies.* And we spend the next couple of hours laughing at the comedy she chooses, content in each other's company and the satisfied purring of Carrot.

CHAPTER SEVEN

WILLOW

"**I**s everything okay?"

Rhys's phone lit up with message after message until he finally excused himself to call the mysterious sender five minutes ago. We've officially been dating for a few weeks, and I still can't believe my luck that Rhys was my match on Luna's app.

He's everything I would've wanted in my dream guy and then some. From his texts to check in on me to the physical command he has over my body and hormones, Rhys is my *heart spark*, I know it. The problem is he doesn't believe in the town legend or really anything that has to do with romantic love, which logically I think I'm fine with because like Shannon said, he shows me how he feels everyday.

But a part of me—the insecure girl who never heard a word of praise or encouragement—is thirsty to hear words of commitment from him. Words of adoration.

You've been reading too many romance novels.

Probably, but does that mean I can't dream of a guy declaring his love for me?

"Everything's fine." Rhys's tone warns against pushing for more details, but my mouth has a mind of its own and questions him anyway.

"Really? Because you kind of seem in a bad mood, and all those messages seemed urgent. You can tell me what's going on. As much as I love that we can joke around, I want us to be able to talk about the serious stuff, too." I try to squeeze his forearm in support, but he backs away, heading for my front door.

"It's just my dad. He heard that my mom will be in town for Hearts Ablaze." He rips his jacket off the coat hanger and shrugs it on, tension vibrating in the air around him.

My brows furrow in confusion. "Why does it matter? Haven't they been separated for years?"

"Pretty much my entire life, but he's still hung up on her. Fucking *heart sparks*, my ass." I know he's pissed over his mom abandoning them and his family trauma, but it still pierces the bubble of happiness I've been living in with Rhys.

There's that need of mine, rearing its greedy head again, despite proof that Rhys doesn't believe in love like me.

"I'll see you later. I need to go talk to him in person." At least he drops a quick kiss on my forehead before hurrying out the door, but it still feels off somehow. Flipping the lock behind him, I sink against the hardwood and stare unseeing into my apartment.

Will what we have now be enough for me?

Can I really just accept actions without words?

I don't know.

STANDING OUTSIDE RHYS'S forge the next afternoon, I channel the spirit of every romance heroine I've ever read, relying on their courage and strength to help me through my plan of seduction.

Hell, Tessa Dare wrote an entire story about a girl falling for a blacksmith with hot sex to boot! I'm just here to live it out in my modern life, right?

Fingers crossed.

This grand idea of seducing Rhys occurred last night when I should've been sleeping, but I couldn't shake the doubts plaguing me about our relationship, especially after hearing his disdain for *heart sparks* again. So, I made a plan.

Rhys and I have fooled around a lot—lord, is he good at it—and my body tingles at just the memory of his touch. But he's always initiating things, and it's time I take charge of my destiny, show him how much I want him, care for him.

Somehow in my mind, I've decided this will help him realize that *heart sparks* are real, and I'm *his*. A flawed thought process, I'm sure, but one I'm going to follow through on, nonetheless.

Because what have I got to lose?

Deep breaths of fresh mountain air fill my lungs, and my feet quickly carry me forward before I lose my nerve. A loud clanking sound travels from the back of the building as I enter, sparks flying from where Rhys is hammering a piece of metal into the perfect shape.

Sweat glistens on his face as shadows from the fiery kiln dance across his large form. He's completely covered in protective gear—long sleeves, safety glasses—but I imagine the bulge of muscles beneath the fabric slick with sweat from the hard labor of his work, and my own body dampens in anticipation of rubbing against this mountain of a man.

My man.

Blowing out a determined breath between my pursed lips, I rub clammy palms down my pink dress and saunter forward as if

I really am the confident heroine of my story instead of scared to death Rhys will find me silly rather than seductive.

"Hey!" Rhys doesn't react to my greeting, so I try again, practically shouting to be heard over the banging of his hammer.

He stops immediately, his chin jerking in my direction, and I flush under his startled gaze. Not quite how I imagined catching his attention—shouting like a fishwife—but at least he's aware of my presence now.

"Willow?" His tools clank to the table as he removes his headgear, swiping a forearm over his gleaming forehead. "What are you doing here?"

I came to seduce you.

"You... What?" Shock tightens his face.

Shit! I said that out loud.

Gotta go with it now.

Gliding forward, I double-check there's nothing molten or burning on the table before sliding between him and the elevated wood, hefting myself onto the tabletop with a whoosh. "You heard me."

God, who is this woman? I don't recognize the confidence in my tone or the brazenness limning my limbs as I spread my legs to accommodate his thick waist.

"Yeah, but I'm having a hard time believing what I heard. What brought this on?" he asks, untying the dirty apron from around his waist. "Not that I don't appreciate the visit." His hands drop to the tops of my thighs, and grayish marks rub off from his skin to mine.

"I figured you could use a pick me up after how we left things yesterday." True, but not entirely the reason. "I don't like how upset you were, and I want to help."

"By fucking me?" A half-smile peeks out behind his beard.

Blushing because he's right, however blunt the assessment, my fingers lower to draw my dress higher until the lace of my panties show. "Exactly. Think of me as a special delivery just for you."

A gravelly chuckle rumbles in his throat before he sweeps the skirt of my dress up and over my head, so my body's on complete display for him.

At least you're wearing your sexy panties this time.

"Sounds good to me." His mouth swoops down to capture mine as one of my arms wraps around his massive shoulders. It's amazing how small he makes me feel, yet powerful, too, like I alone am able to bring him to his knees.

My other hand goes for the button and zipper of his jeans, eager to finally feel his large cock between my thighs. The first time I held him in my palms trepidation shadowed my thoughts—*can we make this work?*—but concern for logistics is the last thing on my mind now. All I want is to be full of him.

"Eager little kitten, aren't you?" he teases, sucking at the pebbled skin around my nipple.

"I think we've waited long enough for this, don't you?" In response, he rips my panties down my legs with a wolfish grin before helping me lower his jeans and boxer briefs enough to free his hard length.

"Oh, I completely agree," he growls. "Sometimes I feel like I've waited forever for you."

I don't have time to bask in the sweetness of the sentiment, despite how it makes my heart clench in hope, because he tosses my legs over his arms and thrusts his cock deep in my pussy without preamble.

"Holy fuck," I whisper, full to the brim with Rhys, burning from the stretch of his thickness.

"Too much?" He acts like he's about to pull out—to gentle himself—but I dig my nails into his arms.

"No, don't stop. It's a lot... *You're* a lot, but you're not too much."

"Good, because my willpower's about to snap. All I want to do is fuck this tight pussy while sucking those bouncing tits of yours. That's why you didn't wear a damn bra today, isn't it?"

Arching my back, I force myself to focus on speaking rather than basking in the sense of rightness, of fullness, at our joining. "Didn't see the point when I planned on stripping for you."

His hips rear back to plunge back roughly, shoving me across the table and disturbing some of his tools with a metal clank. "You sayin' I missed a strip show?"

"Well, I kinda forgot all of my plans the moment I saw you sweating with that hammer in your hand. You're a damn sexy blacksmith." Like if blacksmith calendars were a thing, and he was the main attraction for every month, I'd buy out every store.

"I'll accept your excuse for today, but I want a raincheck."

"You've got it. Now enough talking, more fucking," I pant, feeling my orgasm build to epic proportions. I thought Rhys's fingers were good. His tongue? Mind-blowing. But his dick? That thick length ramming deep and dragging across every nerve-ending?

Yeah, I'm not sure I'll survive it.

Not sure I'll survive him.

"Your wish is my command." Rhys picks up the pace then dips his head to catch one of my nipples with his teeth, nipping and sucking until they're too sensitive, but he refuses to let up.

He fucks me like an animal. Black streaks form on my thighs where he holds me open for his possession, the residue of his work bleeding between us, and I'm hungry for more of his marks.

"Come on, kitten. Work that little pussy of yours. I want your hot cream coating my dick before I fuck you full of me, fill you up until you're dripping with my cum, your thighs sticky with my ownership."

Oh, god.

My body tightens unbearably before a cry of release rises from my chest and pleasure washes over me. Bliss from my orgasm is followed by the warm splash of Rhys coming. *Thank goodness for birth control.* We couldn't even stop to grab a condom before falling onto each other.

Hugging him close, I hum in satisfaction, a zen kind of haze settling over me. My muscles slowly relax, and love for him blooms greater in my heart. It doesn't matter if it's too soon. "And you say you don't believe in love," I tease, trying to catch my breath.

Rhys stiffens in my grasp. "What are you talking about? I don't."

Rolling my eyes, I lazily list all of my points. "You say love's a feeling, but it's *also* an action. One that you're very good at showing. You always check in on me with texts at work. You volunteered to help me run the boutique's booth at Hearts Ablaze last night before your dad messaged, despite calling the entire event, and I quote 'bullshit.' Hate to break it to you, Rhys, but you show love in all the ways that count. Even if you refuse to name it."

"Goddammit." He runs a hand through his hair and backs up, a look of frustration crossing his features. "Are you serious right now?"

The euphoria of my orgasm fades as his rigid demeanor registers. *Shit.* I should've kept my mouth shut, instead of getting all sappy on him. Damn orgasm endorphins. They left me unfiltered, overcome with happiness.

"We agreed to try and understand the other person's point of view," he mutters. "I knew it was too good to be true. Knew you wouldn't be able to resist twisting things around to mean love. To mean those damned *heart sparks*. Every woman I've ever known has done the same thing. What you all fail to understand is that respect or kindness or fucking orgasms doesn't equal love." The last word ends with a spiteful shout, and my body freezes in dread.

"I'm not saying you love me," I backtrack, afraid I've stepped way over the line.

"But you think it'll happen. In your mind, you've rationalized that I'm just working my way towards it, and I'm fucking not. I will fuck you. I'll take care of you. But I am not your *heart spark*. Is that clear?"

"Crystal." Hopping down from the table he just fucked me on, I bat away the tears threatening to fall. *God, this plan was stupid. I'm stupid.* "I've gotta go. Hannah's expecting me for more wedding planning. I'll catch you later."

"Willow..." Regret enters his tone, but it's too late for apologies or retractions. He spoke his truth, whether he meant for it to come out so harshly or not. And he has a right to be angry, I suppose. My words ran away from me. I voiced things I shouldn't have.

The door to his forge slams shut behind me, and I hear the rattle of metal crashing together as another epithet roars from inside.

How could an afternoon that started so well turn sour so quickly?

Because of your big mouth and stupid heart.

CHAPTER EIGHT

RHYS

"So, you fucked it up with Willow, hmm?"

"Hannah told you?"

"Yeah, I got an earful about what an insensitive jerk you are. Thanks for that, by the way." King lightly punches me on the shoulder in retribution. We're in his home office since an urgent problem came up with his job, and I figured I could use a break from my lonely cabin. Especially after the fall out with Willow.

Lifting my chin in apology, the sketch of his and Hannah's wedding bands takes shape on the notepad resting on my knee.

"Let me ask you something I've been curious about for a while," King says, resting his arms on the table covered in folders and loose sheets of paper. "How do you feel about your dad?"

My body jerks in surprise at the random comment. "My dad?"

"Yeah, if you don't believe in love, does that extend to him, too? And if you're not saying 'I love you, Dad,' how do you express yourself otherwise.?"

"That's different. I trust my dad. Respect him. That's enough."

"Seriously?" King scoffs.

A rogue line appears on the band for Hannah, and I roughly erase it. Annoyed by this line of questioning, I admit, "Fine, I love my dad. Are you happy now? But it's not the same. You're trying to get into the semantics of romantic love versus familial love, and it doesn't matter. I may love my dad, but I refuse to love like him. Refuse to believe people have *heart sparks*."

"So this is about your mom."

Tossing my pencil aside, my hand flexes in reaction to his knowing tone. I wish I was in my forge. I wish I had a hammer in my hand to release the sudden rise of chaotic energy in my veins. "What if it is? She's caused enough drama for my family to know I want no part of her beliefs," I spit out. "She called my dad her *heart spark*, claimed to love him, then dumped him for her next true love. While poor Dad still pines for her years later. It's sad and painful, and I'm not falling prey to the same thing."

"First off..." King leans forward, meeting my eyes with his stern gaze. Sometimes I forget that he's a decade older than me, more of an older brother to mentor me rather than a peer going through the same shit I am. "Willow is not your mom. She's sweet and generous and would never abandon the people she loves. Secondly, the fact that you're allowing your mom and dad to dictate your life at thirty years old is ridiculous. Man up, brother. Deal with your emotional baggage then claim your woman."

My eyes narrow at the command. It's easy for King to tell me what to do. He's not the one who has to deal with his father commenting about the lost love of his life constantly. He's not the one who gets a call from Austin every anniversary of milestones they shared—first kiss, birthday, wedding day—where his dad is drunk and melancholic.

"I've dealt with it." He looks at me skeptically. "Fine, I'm a mess. Is that what you want to hear?"

"No, I want to hear you're going after Willow come hell or high water."

"She believes in love and the *heart sparks* shit. That's what she wants. That's what she expects from me."

"So give it to her." King rakes a hand down his grizzled face. "Jesus Christ, it's not like it's a hardship. Loving a woman can be frustrating at times, but it's always worth it. And Willow's one of the best. You're gonna be a coward and lose out on her because of your fucking parents?"

When he puts it like that...

Am I being a coward?

My whole life I've sneered at the idea of love—its meaning worthless after seeing my parents' version of it. But here's King, one of my closest friends, committed and in love to the woman of his dreams. And the guys over at Olson-Keller Lumber... Well, I never thought I'd see the day they settled down, yet all three men are happily married and adore their wives.

Proof of love—of *heart sparks*—has literally been staring me in the face for years. I've just been too stubborn to accept it. And now it might be too late for me to claim it with Willow.

"Shit... I fucked up."

King breathes a sigh of relief and relaxes back into his desk chair. "Yeah, you did. Now what are you gonna do about it?"

CHAPTER NINE

WILLOW

"Figured I'd find you here." A familiar voice calls from the end of the famous Suitor's Crossing bridge. It's Valentine's Day, which means it's decked out to the max with sparkly fairy lights and hearts galore, but the thunderstorm above thankfully prevents the mass of people who'd usually congregate here from visiting. Instead, they moved everything indoors at the community center.

Somewhere I should be to man the boutique's booth, but after explaining my head space, Hannah offered to cover for me. *Thank god for good friends.* Because being surrounded by happy couples on a dreary day that perfectly matches my mood makes my stomach twist in knots, which is why I drove to the bridge, to be alone.

Yet Rhys still found me.

"What are you doing here?" I shout to be heard over the pounding rain bouncing off the wooden roof covering the bridge. He's soaked from the storm—hair plastered to his head, droplets dripping down his beard. He should look like a drowned cat—*a drowned mountain lion more like*—instead of the attractive giant hired to model outdoor gear.

"I came to find you. We need to talk."

"Everything that needed to be said was spoken the day I went to your forge. You made yourself abundantly clear. You'll fuck me, but you won't love me."

He flinches at my harsh words. "I was an idiot." Rhys nears where I'm leaning on the sturdy rail of the bridge and mirrors my bent position, elbows resting on the wood, gaze staring out at the rain dappling the creek beneath us.

"I'm sorry for what I said. I'm sorry for pushing you away." A sigh of regret hovers in the air, and I force my heartbeat to remain steady instead of galloping headfirst into hope. Rhys hasn't mentioned his views on love changing. This could just be an apology, so things aren't awkward between us.

Shrugging in feigned nonchalance, I mumble into the scarf wrapped around my neck and chin, "You did what you thought best. Yeah, it sucked, but it's what you believe. I knew that going into your forge. From the beginning, you were upfront about your feelings."

"Yes, but I was wrong. Afraid of becoming like my dad—pining after a woman who deserted him and their child. Worried I wouldn't be able to discern real love from fake." He turns to face me, and I hold my breath, too scared to trust what I think he's trying to tell me. "But I can't live my life that way. Can't live in fear. Especially when all I want is you—a beautiful, kindhearted woman with a cat who already loves me."

A watery laugh bursts free at his mention of Carrot, my heart swelling with hope. "Does this mean you believe in *heart sparks*? In love?"

He cups my cheek, a tender smile shining back at me. "I believe I could fall in love *with you*. I believe *you* could be my *heart spark*."

And that's enough for now.

After all, we've got time to build a relationship. My mouth may have run unchecked the day at the forge, and love may already fill my heart for him, but I can wait for him to catch up. Because now he's willing to try.

"I accept your apology, and I'm sorry, too. I didn't mean to make you feel cornered, like I expected something from you that you weren't ready for. Blame the great sex that happened beforehand for short-circuiting my brain."

A sly grin overtakes the seriousness tightening Rhys's expression. "Great sex, huh? I'm curious to see what else you say when you're overcome by my cock."

"Oh, lord." Rolling my eyes, my fingers tug at the belt loops of his jeans. "You're gonna be a handful, aren't you?"

"Kitten, I'm twice your size. What do you think?" He doesn't let me answer before his amused chuckle is muffled behind our lips meeting in a final sign of forgiveness.

This kiss feels different than our others. I'm not sure if it's because I know he's open to loving me or if it's due to him finally allowing himself to be vulnerable, freely offering himself to me. Either way, it's magical and full of promise.

One I know will live forever branded on my heart as the perfect Valentine's Day kiss.

A kiss from my *heart spark*.

EPILOGUE ONE

RHYS

This year's Hearts Ablaze is booming with people. After last year's rain out, it's like everyone decided to celebrate doubly to make up for the let down at the community center. Willow's busy writing down a bride's information for an appointment while I man my own booth next door to the boutique's.

My girl talked me into selling some specialty pieces at the festival to drum up extra business—as if I'm not busy enough—but it never hurts to try new things, something I've learned from Willow this past year.

I love her.

Actually... happily... in love.

Something I never thought would happen to me, something I never thought *could* happen to me. But she's shown me how wrong I used to be.

"You really believe in this *heart spark* nonsense?" A guy nears my booth and jerks his finger toward the large tent set up for Suitor's Crossing's legacy of love at the center of the festival.

"Yep." I nod, crossing my arms over my chest.

"Really?" A brow raises skeptically as he glances at the tent again where couples are posing on a replica Suitor's Crossing bridge.

"I'm living proof it exists, and I know others who would say the same. But I understand your doubt. I felt the same way once upon a time."

Willow ambles over to my side after finishing with her bride, and I wrap my arm around her shoulders—she's so tiny compared to me, my arm practically dwarfs her. "I think most people have their misgivings about *sparkin'* and *heart sparks*. It sounds too fantastical to be real until you experience it for yourself," she explains to the stranger. My lips drop to brush a kiss over her temple, and the man shrugs, his hands shoved in his pockets.

"If you say so... Guess I'm happy you two found it."

"Thanks, and I hope you find yours, too." Willow smiles encouragingly, but the man just shakes his head.

"Yeah, I doubt that'll happen but thanks. I actually came over here to ask if you know where I can find the florist's booth? My sister sent me to pick something up for her, but I can't find it in this maze."

Willow points him in the right direction, and soon it's just the two of us... along with the hundreds of people passing by, but I tune them out. "You've been busy this morning."

"So have you," she says, resting her head against my chest. "Told you people would love these metal hearts you made."

"Metal hearts that King has given me nothing but crap about for weeks." He loves to rub it in my face how pro-Valentines and love I am these days.

But as I like to correct him—I'm pro-Willow.

She's my love.
My *heart spark*.

EPILOGUE TWO

LUNA

"How long is this going to take?" My mom's disgruntled question pokes another hole in the bubble of pride I've been floating in since learning the Chamber of Commerce wanted to honor me. After helping multiple local businesses launch their websites, someone nominated me for the Emerging Leaders award, and this morning's chamber meeting is when I'll receive the commendation.

A part of me had hoped my mom would be proud of me—would care that her only daughter is being recognized before the entire town of Suitor's Crossing—but her apparent disinterest proves how wrong I'd been to think this time would be any different than every other time we're together.

"Meetings are usually an hour. I'm not sure when they'll mention the award, though." Most of the attendees are speaking along the edges of the room with cups of the provided hot coffee in hand; no one seems in a particular hurry to start the meeting early since there are still about ten minutes before it's officially slated to begin.

Mom huffs in annoyance and pulls out her phone. "Just remember I have to pick up Bob's groceries at eleven-thirty, so this better not run long. Shouldn't have even come," she mumbles under her breath. "Now you've got me stressed about work."

A guilty flush heats my cheeks as I focus on the bright screen of my own phone, my skin tingling in shame and disappointment. She'd mentioned work when I asked her to come with me last week, but I convinced her to attend anyway, promising it wouldn't interfere with her schedule. Then on the drive here, she brought it up again, deflating my sense of accomplishment even more.

Colors blur on the phone screen as I bite my tongue and rapidly blink away tears. I should have known she'd ruin this for me. Everyone comes before me. Even Bob, a random man in her neighborhood that she somehow agreed to run small errands for. Mom lives off checks from the VA since my dad died, and to make ends meet, she does odd jobs around town when she feels like it.

They're always at strange times and never pressing, but somehow they become a matter of life or death when one happens to fall during a time I need her. Like when I had surgery for my wisdom teeth and needed a ride home—Mom was an hour late picking me up because she wanted to start a load of laundry for a friend. Or when I booked us a mother/daughter spa package for her birthday, and she told me that another friend asked to be driven to the library.

Every errand is vague with "friends" I don't know yet take priority over me.

You were stupid to ask her to come today.

But I'll make the same mistake again... and again—because no matter how many times she lets me down, my optimistic personality refuses to let me quit trying.

A notification appears at the top of my screen, and I eagerly click on it to view my 'Music Year Unwrapped.' I love insights like these, enjoy the snapshot they provide of who I am.

Music starts playing once the app opens, and I hurry to turn down the volume before reading about my top artists and my listening personality. "Hey, Mom, look. They deemed me an 'Out of This World Explorer.' Check out the rest of my traits." I offer her my phone to scroll through the slides.

"No, I don't want to." She rolls her eyes and a grimace tightens her mouth. "When is the damn thing going to start?"

Deflated, I sink back into the chair. It's not a big deal, just a stupid app, but my heart squeezes painfully as if it's a personal affront. Like she doesn't even care to learn this small thing about me.

"Can I see?" A low male voice sounds behind us, and I turn to find Austin Fielding, The Ole Aces bar owner. Scars pucker his face from time spent in the military while his large frame barely fits the small folding chair he's seated in.

"What?"

He motions toward my phone. "Your listening personality. Learning about other people's preferences always fascinates me. Plus the song that was playing is one of my favorites, so I'm curious to see how we match up. But if that's weird or..."

"No!" My body twists to face him more fully, though chamber members are starting to take their seats to start the meeting. "I mean, you can look if you want. Everybody jokes about seeing the repetitive shares on social media, but I like seeing what people listen to, too," I finish dumbly, pausing on the second 'too.'

Try to act normal, Luna.

To be fair, I realize I'm pretty quirky for our small town—everyone thinks I was named after Luna Lovegood from *Harry Potter* due to our similarities—but I'm working on toning it down around strangers. Not that Austin's a complete stranger. I've been to his bar a couple of times and our friends are dating, so we're aware of each other. But he tends to stick to himself.

"I'm Luna, by the way." In case he forgot.

A strange light enters his eyes as his lips quirk upward. "Yeah, I know who you are, Luna."

Oh.

"If we can have everyone's attention, we'll get started," Dr. Avery announces from his center position up front, and the room quiets. Austin returns my phone, his fingertips brushing mine as if we're in slow motion—each pinpoint of his touch eliciting a spark of recognition.

Heart sparks.

No, it can't be.

Suitor's Crossing has a town legend about finding your soul mate or *heart spark*, which I wholly believe is true, but surely Austin can't be mine. We've been in each other's company before and nothing happened. Yes, I find him attractive in a brooding mountain man kind of way, but that's not how *heart sparks* work.

Maybe it just required a touch.

"First order of business..." Another chamber member reads down the agenda as I straighten in my seat, contemplating the burst of electricity I felt between us. Static electricity? Perhaps. But the possibility of discovering my *heart spark* consumes my thoughts the entire meeting.

Overshadowing my acceptance of the award.

Distracting me from my mom's attitude.

Is Austin Fielding the man meant to be mine?
My *heart spark*?

Read *Adored by the Mountain Man* to find out what happens next between curvy Luna and scarred Austin!

THANKS FOR READING & DON'T FORGET TO RATE/ REVIEW!

Please consider leaving a rating/review. Ratings & reviews are the #1 way to support an indie author like me.

The more reviews, the more my books are shown to other potential readers!

And they serve as guides to readers on whether or not to take a chance on an indie author.

I appreciate your support!

XO, Hallie

ABOUT THE AUTHOR

Hallie prefers steamy, insta-love stories where curvy girls are claimed by filthy-talking heroes. And when she ran out of reading material, she decided to write her own stories. If you want a quick, hot read, she's your girl!
Find more about Hallie at halliebennett.com!

www.ingramcontent.com/pod-product-compliance
Lightning Source LLC
Chambersburg PA
CBHW030356180626
46812CB00007B/2911